D0784043

IMAGINE THAT™

Licensed exclusively to Imagine That Publishing Ltd
Tide Mill Way, Woodbridge, Suffolk, IP12 1AP, UK
www.imaginethat.com
Text and illustration copyright © 2019 Cherie Zamazing
All rights reserved
4 6 8 9 7 5 3
Manufactured in China

Written and illustrated by Cherie Zamazing

All rights reserved. No part of this publication may be reproduced, stored in a retrieval system, or transmitted in any form or by any means, electronic, mechanical, photocopying, recording or otherwise, without the prior written permission of the publisher. Neither this book nor any part or any of the illustrations, photographs or reproductions contained in it shall be sold or disposed of otherwise than as a complete book, and any unauthorised sale of such part illustration, photograph or reproduction shall be deemed to be a breach of the publisher's copyright.

ISBN 978-1-78700-908-0

A catalogue record for this book is available from the British Library

Animal Magic

By Cherie Zamazing

'To my mum Elaine for her ever-inspiring imagination, endless love and support and to Nanny and BooBoo for always believing in me.'

Peter loved collecting pebbles – large ones, small ones, thin ones, fat ones, round ones, flat ones! He painted his pebbles to look like all sorts of different animals.

One day, as Peter was putting
his newly-painted fish pebble on the shelf,
he slipped and the pebble SPLOSHED into his fish bowl.

Suddenly, there was a flash
of light and a BUBBLE and a FIZZ!
Peter jumped back and saw a new colourful fish swimming
around the fish bowl. Peter's pebble had come to life!

‘Wow! If my fish pebble came to life in water, maybe my parrot pebble will come to life in the air!’ Peter thought, excitedly.

Peter opened his window
and threw his parrot pebble out into the air!

With a SWISH and a SWOOP,
Peter's pebble came to life!

Peter then picked up his monkey pebble.
'Hmm, monkeys like bananas,' he thought.
So he put the pebble into the fruit bowl!

In an instant, the fruit EXPLODED
everywhere and then ...

A monkey was in the kitchen!

Next, Peter took his crocodile pebble into the bathroom. He filled the bath full of water, and dropped in the pebble. There was a **BUBBLE** and a **SPLASH** and Peter couldn't believe his eyes when a huge crocodile appeared in the bath!

SNAP!
SNAP!

Back in his bedroom, Peter showed the animals his map and pointed out where in the world they normally lived.

Just then, Peter's mum called ...

'Peter! Your dinner is ready!'

'Wait here,'
Peter said to the animals.

While Peter was downstairs, the monkey picked up the rest of Peter's painted pebbles and placed them on the map where Peter had said they lived.

Suddenly, Peter could hear an almighty commotion coming from upstairs. Luckily, Mum and Dad were too busy talking to notice. Peter quickly finished his food and raced back to his bedroom.

Peter gasped when he saw that all of his painted pebbles had come to life!

'I'll get in trouble if you stay here. I need to find a place for you all to live!'

Then, Peter had an idea!

He ran to his cupboard and pulled out a huge pebble. He had been saving it, but he hadn't known what to paint until now ...

Peter waited
until everyone
was asleep and then
led the animals quietly
out of the house and down
to the beach.

Peter climbed into his boat, and together he and the animals swam, rowed and flew out into the ocean.

When they had travelled far enough, Peter lifted the big pebble into the air and threw it with all his might!

Immediately, there was a deep rumbling sound and the boat began to rock as the waves rose higher and higher ...

Suddenly, out of the waves a huge island appeared!
There were jungles full of plants and palm trees,
clear blue streams, waterfalls, mountains
and, of course, a yellow sandy beach,
just as Peter had painted
on his large pebble!

As the sun came up, all of the happy animals waved goodbye to Peter as he rowed his way back home!

'I'll visit you soon!' he called.

As Peter reached the shore,
he spotted a very strange-shaped pebble.
'Hmm, I wonder what I can paint next,' he thought.